My Best Friend

Mary Ann Rodman

Illustrated by

E. B. Lewis

PUFFIN BOOKS

PUFFIN BOOKS
Published by the Penguin Group
Penguin Young Readers Group, 345 Hudson Street, New York, New York 10014, U.S.A.
Penguin Group (Canada), 90 Eglinton Avenue East, Suite 700, Toronto, Ontario, Canada M4P 2Y3
(a division of Pearson Penguin Canada Inc.)
Penguin Books Ltd, 80 Strand, London WC2R ORL, England
Penguin Ireland, 25 St Stephen's Green, Dublin 2, Ireland
(a division of Penguin Books Ltd)
Penguin Group (Australia), 250 Camberwell Road, Camberwell, Victoria 3124, Australia
(a division of Pearson Australia Group Pty Ltd)
Penguin Books India Pvt Ltd, 11 Community Centre, Panchsheel Park, New Delhi - 110 017, India
Penguin Group (NZ), Cnr Airborne and Rosedale Roads, Albany, Auckland 1310, New Zealand
(a division of Pearson New Zealand Ltd)
Penguin Books (South Africa) (Pty) Ltd, 24 Sturdee Avenue, Rosebank, Johannesburg 2196, South Africa

Registered Offices: Penguin Books Ltd, 80 Strand, London WC2R ORL, England

First published in the United States of America by Viking, a division of Penguin Young Readers Group, 2005
Published by Puffin Books, a division of Penguin Young Readers Group, 2007

3 5 7 9 10 8 6 4 2

THE LIBRARY OF CONGRESS HAS CATALOGED THE VIKING EDITION AS FOLLOWS:
Rodman, Mary Ann.
My best friend / Mary Ann Rodman ; illustrated by E. B. Lewis
p. cm.
Summary: Six-year-old Lily has a best friend for play group day all picked out,
but unfortunately the differences between first-graders and second-graders are sometimes very large.
ISBN: 0-670-05989-7 (hardcover)
[1. Best friends-Fiction. 2. Friendship-Fiction.] I. Lewis, Earl B., ill. II. Title.
PZ7.R6166My 2005
[E]-dc22 2004022778

Puffin Books ISBN 978-0-14-240806-3

Manufactured in China
Set in Coop light
Book design by Nancy Brennan

For Lily Nell Rodman Downing and David Eley
—M. A. R.

To the children of the Hammonton Swim Club
—E. B. L.

Today is Wednesday. It's playgroup day at
the neighborhood pool.
That's when I see my best friend, Tamika.
Tamika is bigger than me. She's seven.
She wears her hair in cornrows with beads.
She has a two-piece bathing suit with pink
butterflies and three rows of ruffles.

"Hi, Tamika," I say.

Tamika wrinkles her nose and sticks out her tongue. Then she jumps into the pool with Shanice.

Tamika is my best friend. She just doesn't know it yet.

"Tamika is ignoring me," I tell Mama.

"Tamika is seven and you are six, Lily," says Mama.

"I'll be seven pretty soon," I say.

"But when you are seven, Tamika will be eight," says Mama. "There are lots of other little girls here. Why don't you play with them?"

I don't want to play with other little girls. I want to play with Tamika!

I bet Tamika would like me if I had a two-piece bathing suit.

"Mama, can I have a new bathing suit?" I ask. "Only babies wear suits with a whale on the front."

"Not until you outgrow that one," says Mama. "Plenty of wear left in that suit."

Mama isn't looking too close.

The very next Wednesday, Shanice yells,
"Hey, Whale Girl."

"Who, me?" I ask.

"Yeah, you," says Shanice. "Your be-hind
is hanging out of your suit."

I run to the bathroom and check
in the mirror. Shanice is right.

Next playgroup, I have a new
bathing suit. It is just like Tamika's—
two-piece, with pink butterflies and
three rows of ruffles.

"Hi, Tamika," I say. "See my new bathing suit?"

"That's a baby suit," says Tamika. "I used to have one just like it."

Tamika has a new suit, too. It is a sparkly pink one-piece with circles cut in the sides, like bites out of a cookie.

"I like your new suit," I say. Tamika doesn't hear me. She's pushing Shanice into the baby pool.

"I like your new suit, Lily," says Keesha. Keesha is six, like me. She's nice, but she's not Tamika.

"Thank you," I say. That Tamika! How can I make her be my friend?

I try sharing. I split my Popsicle with Tamika.

She shares her half with Shanice.

I let Tamika borrow my floating noodle. Tamika and Shanice float away, pretending they are mermaids.

That Tamika! If Shanice weren't there, we could be real good friends.

Then one Wednesday, Shanice isn't there.

"Do you want to play mermaids?" I ask Tamika.

"OK," says Tamika.

We have so much fun, Tamika and me. We play mermaids. We slide down the slide. At snack time we share. I give her half of my cherry Popsicle. She gives me half of her grape one.

I am so happy I think I will pop. Tamika is my best friend.

I can hardly wait for next Wednesday.

"Tamika, where are you?" I call when I
get to the pool.
There is Tamika. And Shanice.

"Is that baby still here?"
Shanice yells from across
the pool. "Isn't it time
for your bottle?"

I want to stick out my tongue
at Shanice. Tamika, too. They laugh
and laugh. They think it's funny.

I am not a baby! I am so mad, I jump
into the pool.

"You are a good diver," says
Keesha. Keesha is nice, but she's not
Tamika.

"Thank you," I say. That gives me an idea. Maybe Daddy could teach me how to really dive. Maybe Tamika would like me if I could dive.

Daddy and I work and work. He shows me how to stand, hands over head, feet in the right place.

At first I just fall in, belly first, the way I always do.

Then one day, I do it right! Daddy scoops me up and hugs me. We laugh and laugh. All the time I am thinking I can't wait to show Tamika.

The next Wednesday, I run ahead of Mama.
Tamika is in the big pool with Shanice. They
are standing on their heads underwater.
"Tamika, watch this," I shout.

I stand straight and tall, toes pointing down. I dive, sharp and clean. It is my best dive ever.

I float to the top and look for Tamika. She isn't there. Tamika and Shanice are climbing up the pool ladder.

Tamika didn't see my dive.

"That Tamika," says a voice behind me. "She wasn't even looking."

It is Keesha.

"That Tamika and Shanice," says Keesha. "They think they're so big 'cause they're going into second grade."

"Yeah," I say.

"What's so great about second grade?" Keesha bounces up and down, making little waves.

"Yeah, what's so great about second grade?"
I bounce up and down, too.

"Do you want to play mermaids?" asks Keesha. She smiles so the space in her teeth shows. I wish I had a space in my teeth. Keesha is nice. Who cares if she's not Tamika?

"Nope," I say. "Let's play sea monsters. You got a noodle?"

"Yeah," says Keesha. "A blue one."

Maybe someday, when Tamika is a hundred and I'm ninety-nine, we'll be friends. But until then, Keesha and I will have lots of fun.